Fun Under the Big Top!

Zip! Zoom! Ellyvan and Zooter race through Jungle Junction. Suddenly, Ellyvan stops. He sees a brand new sign!

What does it mean?
"The circus is coming to town!" says Zooter.

The sign leads to Miss Jolly's school.
"We can't wait to see your circus!" says Zooter.

"How would you like to be in my circus?" asks Miss Jolly.

Taxicrab is the circus juggler.
"My juggling is as smooth
as my smoothies!"
says Taxicrab.

The Beetle Bugs are acrobats.
"Ta-da!" cry the Beetle Bugs.

"My two wheels are perfect for the high wire," says Zooter.

But what could Ellyvan do?

"How about the trapeze?" asks Bungo. "You can soar through the air with the greatest of ease!"

Ellyvan closes his eyes and jumps off the platform!

Thud.

"Am I doing it?" asks Ellyvan.
"Not quite," says Bungo.

"How about the seesaw?" asks Zooter.
"You can tumble and twirl!"

The Beetle Bugs jump on the seesaw.
Uh-oh! Ellyvan doesn't budge.

"Am I doing it?" asks Ellyvan.
"Not quite," says Zooter.

"Sorry, Miss Jolly. I guess I'm too big for the circus," Ellyvan says sadly.

Just then, Taxicrab trips and bumps into the tent pole!

Whoa! The tent is falling!

Ellyvan holds up the tent with his trunk! "You saved the day!" says Miss Jolly.

Miss Jolly starts the circus. "Presenting . . . the Jungle Junction Circus!"

Zip zip! The Amazing Zooter rides the tightrope on one wheel!

Hup hup! Taxicrab the Great can juggle anything! Even Toadhog!

Whoosh! Bungo the Magnificent flies over the crowd!

Boing boing! The Bouncing Beetle Bugs build a pyramid!

"And now," announces Miss Jolly, "the strongest strongman in Jungle Junction—Ellyvan!"

"Am I doing it?" Ellyvan asks Zooter.
"You sure are!" says Zooter.

Bravo! The circus stars take their bows!
The Jungle Junction Circus is a big hit!

The End!